Bear Goes Over the Mountain

Characters

Narrator

Birds

Bear

Bees

Trees

Setting

A mountainside in spring

Picture Words

friends

mountain

Sight Words

down	go	I	like
my	see	up	you

side

top

Enrichment Words

back	high
other	over

Narrator: Bear lived on one side of a mountain. Bear had many friends on his side of the mountain.

 Birds: Hi, Bear.

 Bear: Hi, Birds.

 Bees: Hi, Bear.

Bear: Hi, Bees.

 Trees: Hi, Bear.

 Bear: Hi, Trees.

 Narrator: Bear liked his side of the mountain.

Bear: I like my side of the mountain. I like my friends.

 Birds: We like you, Bear.

 Bees: We like you, Bear.

 Trees: We like you, Bear.

Narrator: But Bear thought there must be more to the world than his side of the mountain. He wanted to see what was on the other side of the mountain.

7

Bear: I want to go.
I want to see.

 Birds: Go.

 Bees: Go see.

 Trees: Go up.

 Bear: Okay. Up I go.

 Narrator: So Bear went up
the mountain.

Birds: Up!

Bees: Up!

Trees: Up!

 Bear: I am up high! I am at the top.

 Narrator: Then Bear went down to the other side of the mountain.

 Bear: Down I go. Down, down, down.

Bear: I can see birds! I can see bees! I can see trees!

 Narrator: The other side of the mountain was very much like Bear's side.

 Bear: But I do not see my friends here . . .

 Narrator: So Bear went back over the mountain.

The End